nickelodeon™

SpongeBob SquarePants™

Annual 2015

EGMONT
We bring stories to life

First published in Great Britain in 2014 by Egmont UK Limited,
The Yellow Building, 1 Nicholas Road, London W11 4AN

Created for Egmont by Ruby Shoes Limited.
Activities and story adaptations by Brenda Apsley. Designed by Graham Wise.

ISBN 978 1 4052 7210 0
57517/1
Printed in Italy

BEST FRIENDS FOREVER!

And that includes

YOU!

Contents

Spot Spot

Spot is a purple jellyfish with a big, black spot, who hides in some surprising places! Find **20** of his hiding places in this annual and write a page number in a jellyfish each tim you spot him. The first one has been done for you.

1 6
2
3
4
5
6
7
8
9

10 11 12 13 14 15 16 17 18 19 20

The Epic Story That is ... SPONGEBOB SquarePants

Ben Hur. Jaws. King Kong. Star Wars.

All great epics, but not as great as the amazing undersea drama that is *SpongeBob SquarePants*. Fun, excitement, extreme silliness with friends, neighbours, and one super-bad baddie: Bikini Bottom has it all!

SpongeBob SquarePants

Every epic needs a hero: handsome, brave, daring and ... yellow. Meet the star of the show, **SpongeBob SquarePants**. He is the Krabby Patty fry cook supreme, mean spatula spinner, fearless jellyfisher, all-round good sponge – and everyone's friend.

"Life is fantabulastical!"

Patrick Star

Who does SpongeBob have as his co-star? A pink starfish called **Patrick Star**. He's a star in name only, but someone's got to have him ...

"D'oh ..."

Gary

The sweet little cutie in this all-star lineup is **Gary**, SpongeBob's pet snail and one-word-only co-star.

"Yee-ha!"

Sandy Cheeks

A star sponge needs a pretty leading lady, and SpongeBob's secret crush is **Sandy Cheeks**, sporty squirrel scientist, karate queen and Texas's best pin-up gal.

"I hate you all!"

Squidward Tentacles

SpongeBob's co-worker is **Squidward Tentacles**, a grey octopus with 6 tentacles. He looks a bit gloomy, unless he's making LOUD music with his best friend ... his clarinet.

Who Are You?

Sandy

Squidward

You can be part of the show!

SpongeBob, Patrick, Gary, Sandy or Squidward? Choose a name or make up your own, like ...

PongBob SmellPants

Squidley Tentpole

Batlick Car

Special Guest Star: ....

Mr Krabs

SpongeBob's boss is a red, dollar-grabbing crab called **Eugene R. Krabs**. He loves the smell, look and taste of money, but most of all he loves making and counting it.

"Money, money, money!"

Sheldon Plankton

No epic is complete without a real bad baddie, and SpongeBob's arch rival is the minuscule schemer supreme, **Sheldon Plankton**. He's mean, green and once he has the secret Krabby Patty recipe ... world domination!

"Gimme, gimme!"

Feet!

Grey tentacles, pink stumps, shiny shoes, space boots, a slimy foot.

Count the **SETS** of Feet on pages **8**, **9** and **10**, and colour in the correct number.

1 2 3 4 5 6 7 8 9 10

Now count **ALL** the Feet and circle a number.

1 2 3 4 5 6 7 8 9 10 11 12 13 14 15 16 17 18 19 20

Answers are on page 68.

Clue, Clue, Guess Who?
SPONGEBOB
Match the clues to the Bikini Bottom Friends and neighbours by writing a letter in each pineapple.
a
b
c
d
e
f
g
Answers are on page 68.
1
I own the Chum Bucket. Karen is my computer wife.
Who am I?
2
I calls the Treedome home. Ma airsuit's white.
Who am I?
3
I am pink - I think. I live under a rock.
Who am I?
4
I am an octopus. I live next door to SpongeBob.
Who am I?
5
I want to pass my boating test. I live in a pineapple house.
Who am I?
6
Meow meow meow meow. Meow meow meow meow meow.
Meow meow meow?
Who doesn't have a clue?

The Battle of Bikini Bottom

SpongeBob and Patrick were trying on t-shirts. Patrick's t-shirt said 'Best Friend' and had an arrow pointing at SpongeBob, and SpongeBob's arrow pointed at Patrick.

"Wow! Clothing that announces our feelings for each other! Let's get 'em, Patrick!" said SpongeBob.

But when the assistant arrived to assist them, Patrick started to sob. "You found a new best friend!" he cried, now that the arrow on SpongeBob's t-shirt pointed to the assistant.

When another assistant arrived, Patrick's arrow pointed at her. "No!" he panicked.

"You're not my best friend!"

"We've gotta ditch these," said SpongeBob, ripping off his t-shirt. "They're sending the wrong signals!

We need new outfits to show our best friend-i-ness!"

Then SpongeBob saw some guys wearing old-style soldier outfits. "Like those."

"We dress up and re-enact old battles," a soldier explained. "Like the Battle of Bikini Bottom."

Patrick knew all about that. "A long time ago the town was divided into two groups," he explained. "Those who washed their hands like softies ... and those who had more important things to do. We fought a battle, and WE won our right to wash as we please."

"You don't wash your hands, Patrick?"

asked SpongeBob.

SpongeBob thought back to the time he'd eaten ice cream off Patrick's hand, and let him pick bits of food off his tongue ...

"Never have, never will!" replied Patrick. "Does that bother you?"

"Yes, that does bother me," said SpongeBob,

"Then I guess we can't be friends," said Patrick.

"What are you saying?" asked SpongeBob.

"Do I have to spell it out for you?"

He wrote U R on a wall, then paused, unsure of how to spell NOT MY FRIEND.

"Oh, come on," said SpongeBob. "We can work this out with a can of disinfectant spray."

"No thank you," said Patrick. "I like my various smells and germs."

"But being clean is better," SpongeBob insisted.

"Says you!" said Patrick. "I like dirty!"

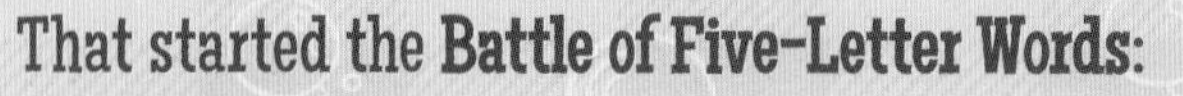

That started the **Battle of Five-Letter Words:**

Then the **SECOND** Battle of Bikini Bottom began. Patrick pulled out SpongeBob's eyeballs, sprayed him with smelly brain juice, then shovelled muck into his tighty-whiteys.

SpongeBob gave Patrick a pedicure, complete with nail polish, and tried to clean his teeth.

Patrick breathed whiffy morning breath over SpongeBob, and pointed his pongy armpits at his ex-friend.

It was all fairly civilised, until SpongeBob chewed a big bar of super-scented soap and fired soap-bullets at Patrick, who emptied the contents of a stinking food-waste-filled skip over SpongeBob.

Patrick ended up shiny, polished and squeaky clean. "My beautiful filth, it's gone!" he wailed. "I'll have to wallow in mud forever to get it back."

"And I'm covered in muck and scum," cried SpongeBob. "I'll need 20 baths a day to get clean. And I'll have to disinfect my eyeballs ..."

"I'll have to slather toe jam on my armpits," said Patrick. "Smear slime on my teeth ..."

DING!

DING! They both realised that those things were just what they liked doing.

"I can spend all day getting **clean**," said SpongeBob. Heaven!

"And now I'm clean I can get **filthier**," said Patrick. Perfect!

"Thanks, SpongeBob," said Patrick.

"No, thank you, Patrick," said SpongeBob.

Battle over, there was only one thing left to say, and they said it ... together:

"You're my best friend ... for ever!"

The End

1, 2, 3, 4, That's What Friends Are For!

Patrick is SpongeBob's **best buddy**, **all-time amigo** and **favourite forever friend**.

They do all kinds of fun stuff together.

Look at these pairs of pictures of the pals and **Spot the Differences** between them.

wide awake

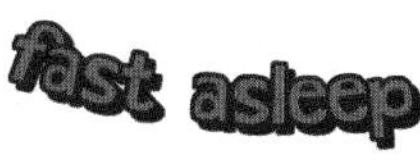

fast asleep

1 Friends ... support each other

a

b

Find 1 difference.

2 Friends ... share tunes
a
b
Find 2 differences.
3 Friends ... bump big bumpy butts
a
b
Find 3 differences.
Answers are on page 68.
4 Friends ... make great dancin' partners
a
b
Find 4 differences.

Come In, Over and Out!
"Come in, come in! Over and out!"
SpongeBob has a message for one of his buddies.
Follow the line from his walkie-talkie to see which buddy he's calling.
a
b
c
d
Answers are on page 68.
18

BE A
JOLLY
JELLY-
FISH

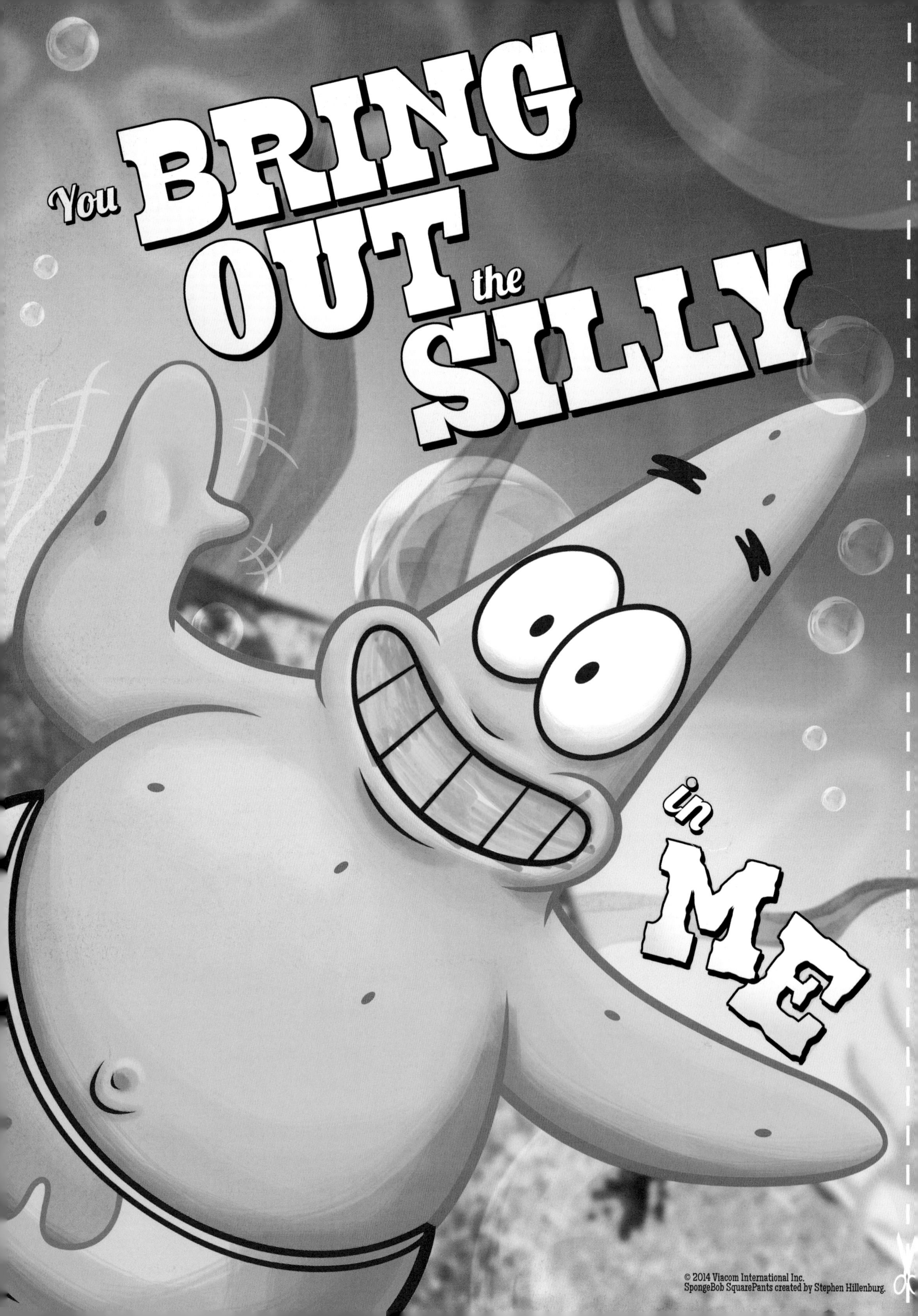
You BRING OUT the SILLY in ME

The SECRET Krabby Patty FORMULA
Plankton's one red eye lights up when he finds a roll of paper labelled:
SECRET FORMULA
"Aha! The Krabby Patty secret formula shall be mine!" he says, unrolling the paper. "But it's written in code, so I have to solve it, then – world domination!"
SECRET FORMULA
Crack the code before Plankton.
Write a letter under each symbol to spell the words, using the picture and letter key at the bottom of the page.
Answers are on page 68.
a b c d e f g h i j k l m
n o p q r s t u v w x y z
SpongeBob
21

Best Buddies

SpongeBob's pals are his all-time best buddies, real friends to the end!

They're the ketchup on his Krabby Patty, and go together like peanut butter and jellyfish jelly!

Tick ✔ each buddy's name you find in the puzzle.

- SANDY
- CHEEKS
- MRS PUFF
- MR KRABS
- GARY
- PATRICK
- STAR

M	C	Z	S	F	Y	Z	M
R	R	P	T	T	X	L	R
S	T	G	A	R	Y	R	K
P	A	T	R	I	C	K	R
U	S	A	N	D	Y	D	A
F	J	P	G	O	M	E	B
F	Q	C	H	E	E	K	S

Answers are on page 68.

Who is your best buddy?

Write a name and draw a picture.

My BFF is:

....

Sea-veillance!
ALERT!
Security camera malfunction!
The residents of Bikini Bottom are under the watchful eyes of sea-veillance cameras that record their every move.
1
2
3
4
5
6
7
8
Answers are on page 68.
ne camera shot has broken up.
This is what the picture should look like:
Put the picture back together by writing a number in each section.

I Spy!

SpongeBob loves playing games wih his friends!

Here's a favourite from his Fun Games File ...

Play **I Spy** with a friend.

Take turns to choose something, then say: "I spy with my little eye, something beginning with ..." and say the first letter of your choice, like **n** for **net**, or **h** for **hat**.

But **don't** say the word!

You could choose one of these items, or something completely different.

Your friend has to guess what you chose. If he or she guesses correctly, it's his or her turn to choose.

If they don't guess, you choose another word.

SECRET FORMULA

GARY

6

JELLYFISH
JAM
BAND
KELP

SPYBOB

Mr Krabs opened his safe to check that the secret Krabby Patty formula was still inside. "Plankton hasn't tried to steal the formula in over a month," he told SpongeBob. "He must be planning something big. I need someone to spy on him."

That someone was SpongeBob.

"Spy?" said SpongeBob. "Whooo! Patrick, I'm gonna be a spy."

"I wanna be a spy, too!" bellowed Patrick.

"Sshh!" Mr Krabs shushed. "Okay, okay, you can be a spy. Just be quiet!"

"Hoooray! We're Spy Buddies!" yelled SpongeBob and Patrick.

Mr Krabs gave SpongeBob his instructions on a Krabby Patty that delivered a recorded message:

YOUR MISSION IS TO DISCOVER WHAT PLANKTON IS UP TO.
DON'T LET HIM OUTTA YOUR SIGHT.
IF YOU DON'T ACCEPT THIS MISSION ...
YOU'RE FIRED!
THIS PATTY WILL SELF-DESTRUCT IN 10 SECONDS.

"Ooooh! Get rid of it, Patrick," panicked SpongeBob.

Patrick found the perfect place to put the exploding patty ... down the front of his shorts!

Ka-boom!

"That's gonna leave a mark ..." said Patrick.

SpongeBob and Patrick spied Plankton buying baby clothes in size negative 5 (the only size small enough to fit him). Then he bought a stamp.

SpongeBob reported back to Mr Krabs, who wrote BABY CLOTHES and STAMP on his spy board. "This is the most elaborate scheme ever," he said. "Keep on him, SpongeBob."

But that was easier said than done, so SpongeBob and Patrick roared off on their jet pack to search for him. But when the thrusters went out of control it destroyed most of Bikini Bottom before crash landing.

Time for the Spymobile. Patrick pressed a button to get it started. The wrong button. The one marked **SELF DESTRUCT!**

KA-BOOOOOOOOOOM!

As SpongeBob and Patrick recovered, Patrick's shorts quivered and a call came in on his pants-o'-phone. "Krabs to Agent SpongeBob. Have you found out what Plankton's up to?"

"Er, we lost him," SpongeBob reported.

Maybe Plankton was in the Chum Bucket. The Spy Buddies climbed onto the roof to check.

"I think the front door's open," said Patrick.

"Spies don't use the front door," said SpongeBob. "We've got to find a complicated way to get inside."

"Looks like a job for Patrick Star Laser Pants," said Patrick.

He bent over, pointed his Laser Pants and cut a hole in the roof.

"Aaaarrgh!"

Then SpongeBob let himself down on a rope. A rope he thought Patrick was holding. **Wrong.**

"Aaaarrgh!"

"Quiet!" yelled Patrick. "We're on a secret mission."

"Secret mission, eh?" snickered Plankton.

He sat the spies at a table and gave them menus.

But Patrick was having trouble with his Laser Pants. They were making strange noises. "I have to go," he told SpongeBob. "My pants aren't working right. I have to go **NOW!**"

Too late. Patrick's pants rumbled, then exploded, and –

Squelch!

Squish!

Sploosh!

BOOM!

no more Chum Bucket.

"This is war!" cried Plankton. He flew his airship to the Krusty Krab and drove all the customers away by playing extra-loud ear-popping music.

When Mr Krabs fired a cannonball at the airship, Patrick leapt off it, but landed in the cannon, and was fired right back.

Rip!

Pop!

Boooooom!

What was left of the airship flattened the Krusty Krab. As the dust settled, "I win! I always win!" cried Plankton.

SpongeBob was just about to point out that he had actually lost when Plankton tore off his skin to reveal ... Mr Krabs!

He explained. "Plankton's been trying to steal the Krabby Patty formula for twenty years. He's never done it. Last time he failed, we made a bet. I said if I was you, I could steal it first try. So we swapped lives. I became Plankton. And I beat him. I stole me own formula. Ack, ack, ack!"

Mr Krabs will do anything to make an extra dollar. **Anything.**

"Ack! Ack! Ack!"

What's Next?
#1 GRILL MASTER BIKINI BOTTOM
SpongeBob is cooking up a Krabby Patty mega-treat of a feast that makes his buddy Patrick drool, slurp, dribble ...
Draw which two items come next in each line.
KRUSTY KETCHUP
KRUSTY KETCHUP
Draw funny faces on the lollies so lolly SpongeBob has some friends.
30

Smile, Please!

"Smile, please, SpongeBob!" Patrick took lots of happy-snap photos of his super-smiley friend to remind them of the fun they had on their Best Buddies trip.

The photos look the same, but one is different. Which one?

Answers are on page 68.

Attach your photo or draw your smiley face.

Krabby Patty Cook Out
Mr Krabs' latest money-making idea is a Krabby Patty Cook Out!
The barbie's burnin' hot, SpongeBob's spatula is on fire, and the patties are flippin' high.
Come and get it!
Count the Krabby Patties ...
THE KRUSTY KRAB
COOK OUT
1
up in the air
2
in a Patrick-size mouthful
KISS THE COOK
3
in the mega-stack
Answers are on page 68.
Awe-sum
Do the sum and write the number

SpongeBob

SMARTYPANTS

The best birthdays are the ones **shared** with friends. SpongeBob always makes a special birthday card for his mega-mate Patrick.

PATRICK

Check out the arty alphabet he used to write Patrick's name on this year's card.

A B C D E F G H I J K L M N
O P Q R S T U V W X Y Z

Copy letters to write the name of your Bestie For Restie.

SpongeBob StoryPants

Sharing fun with friends and neighbours and making buddies feel good are what life in Bikini Bottom is all about. Remember these great storylines?

Tea at the Treedome

SpongeBob meets his new friend, Texan squirrel Sandy Cheeks for the first time. It's a love-fest!

Help Wanted

SpongeBob's best friend Patrick encourages him to apply for a job at the Krusty Krab, and when he feeds a sea of hungry anchovies, the job is his. His dream has come true!

Jellyfishing

After Squidward has an accident, SpongeBob and Patrick decide to cheer up their friend by giving him his Best Day Ever, and take him jellyfishing with them.

Home Sweet Pineapple

When parasites wreck his pineapple house, SpongeBob's good friends offer him a place to stay. But they soon find that SpongeBob may be a great buddy, but he's not easy to live with.

Naughty Nautical Neighbours

Squidward plays a joke on SpongeBob and Patrick, making them think they are no longer friends. But the joke backfires on Squidward when Patrick and SpongeBob both compete to be HIS new best friend.

Your Shoe's Untied

When Patrick can't tie his shoelace, he turns to his best friend SpongeBob for help. But he's forgotten too, so it's up to Gary to show them how it's done.

Walking Small
Plankton tries to make SpongeBob act mean, but he just can't do it. it's much more fun being nice, and you get to make more friends that way.
Fungus Among Us
SpongeBob catches an itchy sea fungus called ick. Like any good friend would, he passes it on to everyone at the Krusty Krab, and it takes one hungry super-hero-snail to save his friends.
The Chaperone
Like a true friend, SpongeBob offers to take Pearl to the dance. When he tries to make himself tall, dark and handsome, Pearl sees what a great mate he is.
The Lost Mattress
Mr Krabs' mattress is lumpy, so SpongeBob, Patrick and Squidward do what any kind friends would do and get him a new one. But it's where Mr Krabs hid his money!
Boating School
Mrs Puff and SpongeBob are good friends, because they see an awful lot of each other ...
RULES of the ROAD
Boating Test 1
FAIL!
Boating Test 562
FAIL!
Boating Test 1,984
FAIL!
Boating Test 4,509
FAIL!
Boating Test 8,611
FAIL!
Boating Test 11,749
35

It's All in the Details

It's fun competing against your buddies in the SpongeBob Games.

THE SPONGEBOB GAMES
DIVING

1

Take a look at these pictures.
A close look.
A **real** close look.

Tick ✓ **only** the details that are in the big pictures.

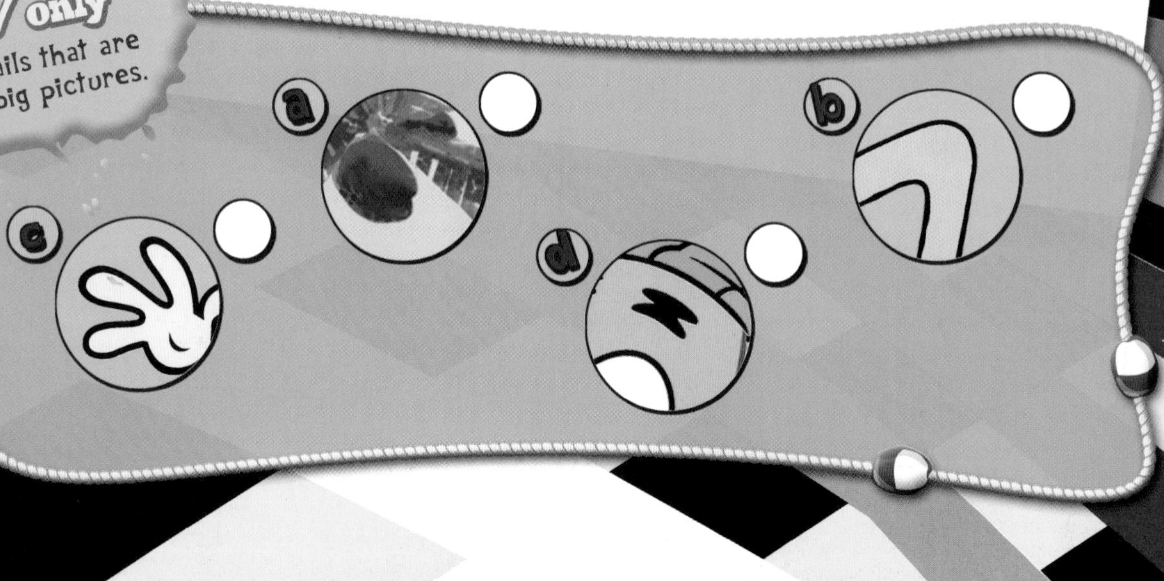

a

b

c

d

THE SPONGEBOB GAMES
RUNNING
2
KELP
1765
KELP
101
KELP
297
Answers are on page 68.
a
b
c
d
e
f

Team
Players
SpongeBob is encouraging his friend Patrick to try out for the cheerleading team. Unfortunately, he's just found out that it entails...
eek! ... doing the splits!
WIN
Make some pompoms so you can cheer along with Patrick.
Ask an adult to help!
You need: red crepe paper
safety scissors
sticky tape
1
For each pompom, cut out a piece of paper 30cm x 1m long.
2
Make 10cm cuts 3cm apart along the top and bottom edges.
3
Roll the paper up tightly and fix in place with sticky tape.
Get shaking!
BB

SpongeBob
FootiePants
Get a Kick Out of This!
SpongeBob and Patrick make a great team, playing together as twin strikers in the Bikini Bottom All Stars.
Find 2 Footballs that are the same.
a
b
c
d
e
f
g
h
i
j
Design new shirts for the Bikini Bottom All Stars.
Answers are on page 63.
39

Have You Seen This Snail?

SpongeBob was just about to feed his pet snail, Gary, when a package arrived.

"My **Mermaid Man and Barnacle Boy** paddleball set!" he yelled. "Hoooooo! And what's this? Take the **Dirty Bubble Challenge**. Hit the ball 29,998,559,671,349 times in a row."

How could SpongeBob refuse a challenge like that? No how, that's how!

But it wasn't easy, and each time SpongeBob hit the ball, the ball hit SpongeBob back. In the eye. Ouch!

HIT. "Darn it." HIT. "Darn it." HIT. "Darn it."

Gary was hungry, so he tried to remind SpongeBob about his food. "Meow!"

The ball hit SpongeBob in the eye again. "Darn it."

SpongeBob ignored Gary, so he meowed louder.

"Meow!"

That got SpongeBob's attention. "I can't play with you right now, Gary," he said.

But Gary tried again.

"Huh! Pets!" said SpongeBob.

The Challenge went on and on and on.

Minutes. Hours. All day. All night.

When Patrick finally persuaded SpongeBob to take a break, SpongeBob fell over Gary's (empty) (fly filled) (pongy) food bowl nd remembered something.

"I **gotta** feed Gary!" he yelled.

But where was Gary?

Gary was gone. Absent. No longer present. Missing. **Away.**

"Er, how long was I taking the Challenge?" SpongeBob asked Patrick.

"About a week, maybe ten days," said Patrick.

Oh, no ...

SpongeBob called Gary's name,

Then he shook a can of Gary's fave treats, nd searched everywhere, even in Squidward's occupied) bath.

He found soap. Suds. A sponge. Squidward. But no Gary.

Then SpongeBob found a letter in his mailbox.

I must move on. Don't bother to come looking for me. I have probably found a new owner who remembers to fill my food bowl.

Gary.

"What have I done?" cried SpongeBob.

"Gareeeeeeeeeeeeee!"

Gary did find a new home, with a little old lady called **Gramma**, who mistook him for one of her ex-pets, and renamed him **Miss Tuffsy**.

He got his own room, music, movies, even a goodnight kiss in his cot. And Gramma fed him on **cookies**.

And **eggs**.

And **popcorn**.

And ...

While Gary was being fattened up, SpongeBob searched for him.

He played his **Gary Come Home** song and put up posters all over Bikini Bottom.

Then he handed out hundreds of **MISSING** flyers asking if anyone had seen his snail.

Thanks to Gramma's force-feeding, Gary was full. Stuffed. Gorged. Ready to explode.

"**Barf!**" he barfed weakly.

"**Muuuurrrooowww ...**"

"**Oh**, do you have to go potty?" Gramma asked him. "Here, use this big stack of flyers a yellow boy gave me."

Gary saw his picture, and read SpongeBob's message. It said:

Gary decided to go home. But when he opened a cupboard to get his things, a heap of **snail shells** fell out on him. **Empty** snail shells. Gramma's ex-pets. Gramma's **EATEN** ex-pets.

"Meow?"

Now Gary is no ordinary snail. No, he has a one-word vocabulary and can even tie shoelaces. So he had no trouble working out what was about to happen to him. As soon as he was fat enough, he was going to be Gramma's next meal. **Snail Soup. Snail Sausage. Snail Soufflé. Gary Gravy!**

Gary made his escape.

By now SpongeBob was a blubbering mess. "Gary ..." he sobbed.

"Meow!"

"If only I could hear you meow," said SpongeBob.

"Meow!"

"Yeah, like that," said SpongeBob. It sounded just like Gary.

"Meow!"

It sounded like Gary because it **WAS** Gary! SpongeBob looked around and saw his pet.

"Meow!"

"Gareeeee!"

Gary was found. Saved. Back where he belonged.

SpongeBob was thrilled. "I promise things are gonna be different," he said. "Let's get home and get you something to eat. You must be **STARVING**!"

Gary groaned ...

"Mrrr-owwwwwwwwwwww!"

The End

Where's Gary?

When Gary escaped from Gramma just before he exploded, he was very pleased to go back home with SpongeBob – until his loving owner tried to feed him up, too! So he slime-trailed off again.

Find Gary. His picture is on SpongeBob's sign.

Answers are on page 69.

Gone Fishin'

Question: What do SpongeBob and Patrick love best, apart from each other?

Answer: Jellyfishing in the Jellyfish Fields – even if it means getting stung!

Jellyfish Fields

Draw and colour in jellyfish, seahorses and corals in the Jellyfish Fields.

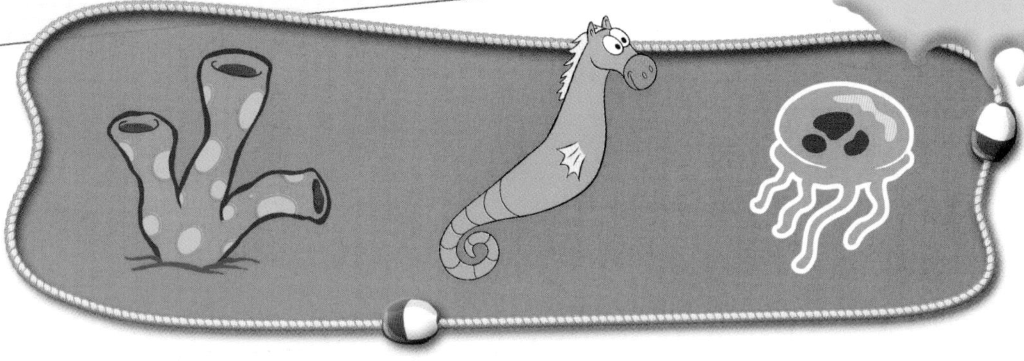

Ride The Wave

What makes SpongeBob and Patrick smile happy smiles like these?

Surfing the waves with their best buddy, that's what!

It's totally wavetastic!

Draw the boarders square by square, and colour in.

ON, GARY!
NORTH POLE
OR BUST!

SPONGEBOB
GO WITH THE FLOW

The SpongeBob Games

Will SpongeBob and Patrick triumph at the deep-sea sports games?

hey both love winning, but they know it's not just the thrill of winning gold medals that's important, it's the taking part, and being part of the Bikini Bottom team.

Draw lines to match the sports and medals.

Answers are on page 69.

Jellyfishing
SpongeBob and Patrick love jellyfishing together! But every trip is a contest. Who will be the first hunter to catch 10 jellyfish?
Play as one of the friends to find out.
TIP: use buttons or coins.
Put SpongeBob and Patrick counters on START.
Take turns to roll a dice. If you roll 2, move 2 spaces, and so on.
When SpongeBob or Patrick land on a jellyfish, use a pencil to shade in a jellyfish in their net.
The first to catch 10 wins!
If SpongeBob or Patrick land on ...
they go on 2 spaces
they go back 1 space
they have an extra throw
they miss a turn
START
TIP: Rub out the pencil to play again.

Let's Go, Buddy

There are lots of things SpongeBob needs to pack for his road-trip vacation.

Seabears!
"Do you see 'em?" Patrick is looking for seabears on Day 1 of his Bond with Your Best Buddy trip with SpongeBob.
Take a look and answer these questions.
1 Count the red seabears.
2 Count the green ones.
3 How many seabears altogether?
BIKINI BOTTOM PARK SERVICE
SEABEAR SPOTTER
Answers are on page 69.
53

Wild!
On Day 2, Patrick takes SpongeBob on a hike.
But Patrick isn't the ocean's greatest map-reader, and thanks to him, they're a little bit lost.
This way! That way! Which way?
Draw a picture map to help Patrick.
From START HERE Follow the arrows
up↑ down↓ left← right→
Draw pictures in the map boxes the arrows take you to.
BIKINI BOTTOM PARK SERVICE
START HERE
Answers are on page 69.
←2 ↑2 →4 ↓1
←2 ↑3 →3
→2 ↑2 ←4
←2 ↑3 →1
→2 ↑3 ←2 ↓1
→2 ↑2 ←1 ↓1
54

A-mazing
"You lead the way, buddy!"
Day 3 of SpongeBob and Patrick's buddy trip has been long and hard, and they need a rest.
Their tent is in Sand Mount Camp Ground.
But, uh-oh, where is that exactly?
Help them both find a path to the tent.
START
START
Answers are on page 69.
"My brain hurts!"
55

The Gift of Gum

It was Best Friends Day, and Patrick had a special gift for SpongeBob.

"This chewing gum is my most beloved possession," said Patrick. "I'm giving it to my bestest friend on Best Friends Day."

"Patrick, I am truly honoured," said SpongeBob. "Sob, sniff, sob ..."

"What's wrong, buddy?" asked Patrick.

SpongeBob couldn't help crying. "You ... sniff ... got me such an ... snuffle ... amazing ... blub ... gift, and all I got you was – THAT !!!"

THAT !!! was a robot. A talking robot.

"GREE-TINGS. I AM RO-BO 2.1, YOUR PER-SON-AL RO-BOT SER-VANT. I AM PRO-FI-CIENT IN PRO-VID-ING O-VER 250,000 CREA-TURE COM-FORTS. WOULD YOU CARE FOR A PAS-TRY?"

Patrick certainly would! "Ooh!" he gushed. "SpongeBob, this is a great gift."

"Oh, thanks, Patrick," said SpongeBob. "But it's no giant, old, used, ball of gum."

"Aw, don't be so hard on yourself," said Patrick. "I love my gift. In fact, I'll go play with it right now. C'mon, Robo."

"COM-ING, MIS-TER PAT-RICK," said Robo.

SpongeBob took Gummie home. He tried to roll him into his house, but it was a struggle. "Hurrrrr! You sure are a big boy, aren't cha?" gasped SpongeBob. "Ooooo! Hey, I know how to handle this – with a little ka-ra-tay!"

HI-YA!

That didn't go to plan, and Gummie ended up on top of SpongeBob.

When SpongeBob finally shoved Gummie inside, he filled the whole room. "Phew!" said SpongeBob. "Gummie, you're a great centrepiece with your ...

... dirty sock

... used toothbrush

... bugs

... and mouldy pizza."

The smell was just terrible, and when a pair of grubby tighty-whiteys escaped from deep inside the gum and spoke to him, SpongeBob decided that Gummie had to go.

He rolled Gummie outside and wedged him into the trash can. "Goodbye, Stinkball, see ya never!" he yelled, then noticed that Patrick was back.

"Watcha doin'?" asked Patrick.

"HE IS THROW-ING GUMM-IE A-WAY," said Robo, helpfully.

SpongeBob put the trash can lid on Gummie. "No," he said. "I just decided to dress him up. Cute, hey?"

When Patrick left to look for belly button lint, SpongeBob dug a big hole to put Gummie in ... but Patrick turned up again.

"I was digging a hole to see Gummie better," SpongeBob explained.

Patrick decided that Gummie would look even better over SpongeBob's front door, and stuck him up there.

Patrick left to learn how to use a fork, and SpongeBob dressed up as a burglar. The plan was to steal Gummie.

But Gummie didn't want to be stolen, and sucked SpongeBob into the goo:

SUUUUCK! SSSLURRRRRRRP!

"Looks like I got myself into a sticky situation," said SpongeBob when Sandy came along.

Sandy tried to help. When a truck drove by, she lassoed it with a long strand of sticky gum. The engine strained, but it was no match for Gummie, and when the truck split in half, the back end got gummed to SpongeBob's house.

RIP! SPLOSH! SPLAT!

SPLOOOOOSH!

Patrick came back again. "What have you done?" he asked when he saw the gummy mess that was SpongeBob's house, Squidward's house, and the rock he lived under. "It's ... amazing!" said Patrick. "It's like a gummie wonderland. Wheeeee! I knew you'd love it. Gee, everyone is having fun with Gummie but me."

Ding! Idea! "Patrick," SpongeBob asked, "do you miss Gummie? It's still Best Friends Day, so would you like your Gummie back?"

"Urrrr ... yes!" yelled Patrick.

"It's yours, buddy," said SpongeBob. "But you gotta get us out of this."

"Ha, that's easy," said Patrick, and he started to suck and chew huge mouthfuls of Gummie goo-gum.

SUCK. SLURP. CHEW. CHOMP. SWALLOW.

URRRP!

"Told ya it was easy," said Patrick.

When Gummie was gone and Patrick was the size Gummie had been – "Hic! Hic! Hic!" – Patrick blew a huge pink bubble that grew ...

and grew until it sat like a vast pink cloud floating over Bikini Bottom. Then – Pop! Splurge! – the cloud burst, and Bikini Bottom was coated in thick, sticky, icky, pink, gummie goo.

"Hic!" Patrick hicced happily. "This is the best Best Friends Day ever!"

The End

Sponge in Space

When SpongeBob journeyed into deep space, he met up with some very weird new buddies on his space-vacation ...

Plankton's relatives get everywhere!

Draw more little pink Pinktons to make 6 altogether.

"Who are you calling weird?"

Christmas is Magic
Christmas is a merry, magical time for sharing fun with family, friends and pets.
Check out this year's Christmas tree!
Christmas is the season to be ... bubbly.
Join the dots.
5
6
7
4
3
8
9
10
2
1
4
5
6
7
3
2
1
8
9
10
8
6
7
9
5
1
3
4
2

SEAson's Greetings
Patrick loves making paper snowflakes at Christmas time. He puts them on cards to send to his friends, and uses them to decorate his Rock house.
You need: white paper safety scissors
Ask an adult to help!
1
Cut out a square of paper 20cm x 20cm.
2
Fold in half to make a triangle.
3
Fold 3 more times, making a smaller triangle each time.
4
Make little cuts along 3 sides.
5
Unfold carefully.
If Patrick had a nose, that would tickle it!

Patrick put a snowflake on his cards.
This one's for you, so write your name on it.
SEAson's Greetings to
Gotcha! Catching snowflakes is almost as much fun as jellyfishing!
Which 2 snowflakes are the same?
a
b
c
d
e
f
Answers are on page 69.
65

Quiz Questions
It's time for a SpongeBob quiz!
How carefully did you read this annual?
All the answers are somewhere in the pages!
1
What 2 things are in the gum Patrick gave SpongeBob on Best Friends Day?
Rearrange the letters.
cosk
zipza
2
SpongeBob works at the Chum Bucket.
TRUE or FALSE
3
Who is the karate queen of Bikini Bottom?
a
b
c
4
Find Squidward's shadow.
a
b
c
5
What is the name of SpongeBob's boating teacher?
66

6
Which is Patrick's nose?
a
b
c
7
When Gary left home, who adopted him?
a Gramma
b Granpa
c Gummie
8
SpongeBob lives in a mango house.
TRUE or FALSE
9
What is this critter?
a a see-saw
b a seabear
c a seasnail
Answers are on page 69.
10
Who showed SpongeBob and Patrick how to tie their shoelaces?
a Sandy
b Gary
c Plankton

Answers

6-7 Spot Spot

Spot is hiding on pages 6, 8, 13, 14, 16, 24, 30, 31, 33, 34, 37, 39, 45, 51, 52, 60, 61, 62, 64 and 66.

10 Feet!

There are 7 sets of feet.

There are 13 feet altogether (Gary has 1).

11 Clue, Clue, Guess Who?

1.g. 2.f.
3.e. 4.b.
5.c. 6.d

Mr Krabs doesn't have a clue.

16-17 1, 2, 3, 4, That's What Friends Are For

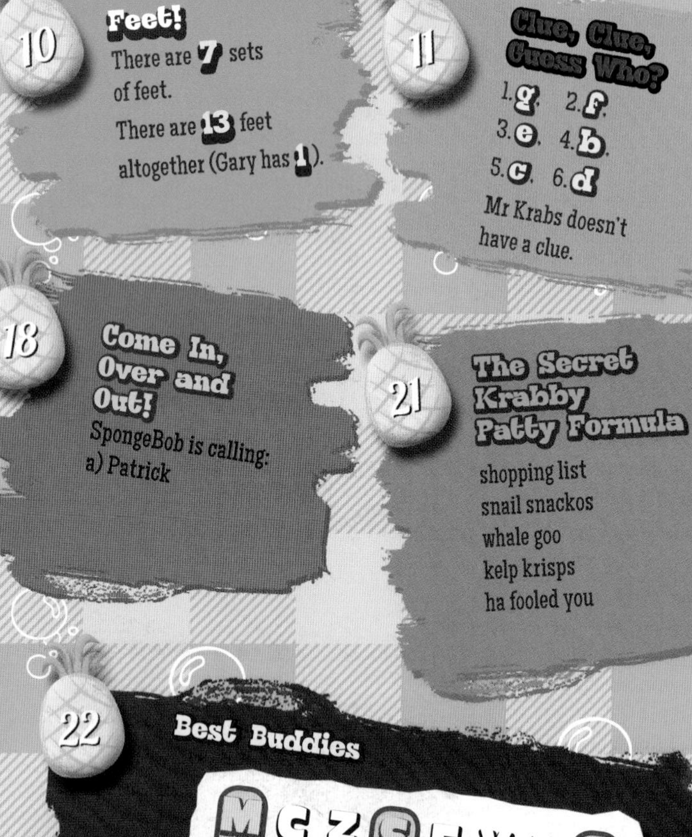

18 Come In, Over and Out!

SpongeBob is calling:
a) Patrick

21 The Secret Krabby Patty Formula

shopping list
snail snackos
whale goo
kelp krisps
ha fooled you

22 Best Buddies

28 Sea-veillance!

31 Smile, Please!

Photo b is the odd one out.

32 Krabby Patty Cook Out

1.5, 2.8, 3.12

Awe-Sum

8 + 6 = 14

36-37 It's All in the Details

1.a d
2.b d e

39 SpongeBob FootiePants

Footballs a and i are the same.

44
Where's Gary?
e.
49
The SpongeBob Games
1. b. 2. d.
3. a. 4. c.
53
Seabears!
1. 4. 2. 3.
3. 9.
54
Wild!
BIKINI BOTTOM PARK SERV
START HERE
55
A-mazing
Here are 2 ways through the maze.
START
START
61
The Boo Crew
62
Scary!
a. c. g. i. k.
65
SEA-son's Greetings
b and f.
66-67
Quiz Questions
1. sock, pizza
2. FALSE, he works at the Krusty Krab.
3. c. Sandy
4. a
5. Mrs Puff
6. It's none of them – Patrick doesn't have a nose!
7. a. Gramma
8. FALSE, he lives in a pineapple house.
9. b. a seabear
10. b. Gary
SpongeBob and Patrick are
Besties for Resties.
Colour in the picture.